T0147464

# THE ROYAL RUBY

## BY

## LITTLE FAWN WHITECEDAR

WESTBOW
PRESS

A DIVISION OF THOMAS NELSON

WestBow Press books may be ordered through booksellers or by contacting:

WestBow Press
A Division of Thomas Nelson
1663 Liberty Drive
Bloomington, IN 47403
www.westbowpress.com
1-(866) 928-1240

Because of the dynamic nature of the Internet, any web addresses or
links contained in this book may have changed since publication and
may no longer be valid. The views expressed in this work are solely those
of the author and do not necessarily reflect the views of the publisher,
and the publisher hereby disclaims any responsibility for them.

Any people depicted in stock imagery provided by Thinkstock are models,
and such images are being used for illustrative purposes only.

Certain stock imagery © Thinkstock.

ISBN: 978-1-4497-3435-0 (sc)
ISBN: 978-1-4497-3434-3 (e)

Library of Congress Control Number: 2011963006

Printed in the United States of America

WestBow Press rev. date: 2/28/2012

# TABLE OF CONTENTS

Coming soon (Look for White Cedar to be published soon by Little Fawn Whitecedar)

## Dedication

This story is a gift given to me straight from
heaven. I want to thank my God for it.
I am thankful to my husband, Gary, who has prayed for and
encouraged me during publication. Also through this process
a good friend of mine, from the country of the Ukraine,
went to be with the Lord. Alisa Shinova helped me with the
historical and geographical aspects of this story. Though
saddened at her passing, I am joyful she is in a better place.
I would also like to thank my daughter Amy who was first
to financially back this venture! Also my daughter Annie
and son Joshua, who I bounced ideas and sketches off of.
To share this story with the world has been
my heart's desire for a long time.

# Chapter 1

## A Place to Hide

Cobblestone streets meandered through the silent picturesque village of 1939 Kanev, Ukraine, with the only sound that night being the rushing waters of the Dnieper river flowing near by. Moonbeams filtering down from the starlit panoramic April sky into each fire lit home promised a peaceful evening.

Out of the silence arose the pounding of a hundred boots stomping out a rhythmic canter that grew louder and louder. With their approach echoing off the stone huts that lined the streets, candlelit homes were suddenly darkened with one breath of each resident. The townspeople knew the familiar sound of the German soldiers that brought great fear to each heart.

Much scurrying and shuffling around in a blind frenzy brought Bogdon to his knees, feeling for the small woven rug that hid the trapdoor in the middle of his three-room home. In darkness he quickly pulled the rug from the center of the floor and said, "Quick children, hide here."

"Thank you Papa," came the small skittish voice of the youngest Jewish refugee, only five years old.

"Please, no talk, just hide!" His whisper grew louder.

Anxious eyes met in the moonlit cabin with each child that was ushered away to the dank, dark cellar beneath the floor boards . Four children in all, not one dared to speak or move once settled there. They knew the routine by now. Seven months had passed since they were taken in by this tender, loving, brave couple. The children had lost their parents in a similar house raid.

Svetlana stood in the darkness with wide-eyed worry and wrung her hands. Her hair fell astray from under her babushka.

She tightened her jaw and made her way to the window, only to hear the loud voices of the SS Officers shouting commands in a foreign language. Her heart sunk into the pit of her stomach. "Bogdon," she whispered. "They approach. Are all the children safe?"

"*Da*, they are" he assured her. He finished placing the rug back in the center. His rugged hand reached around the thin frame of Svetlana, giving a reassuring hug, and for a moment, there was a peace for both of them. Then a sudden jolt of remembrance that they needed to hide the children's shoes by the door, and other tell tale items that would surely give away the fact that there were unauthorized children in the home.

Nearer and nearer, the thunderous sound of the clamping boots permeated through their very souls. More scurrying and bumping around in the dark until they were satisfied that no item was left out. The echoing howl of a nearby dog gave an eerie chill down their spines. Distant sinister sounds resonated ever closer. Loud commands, boots ceasing, one silent moment and then…

Bang! Bang! Bang! The door flung wide open and there stood a tall dark shadow of an SS soldier. The elongated military overcoat framed his massive body and faded into the pitch of the night. The swastika on his shoulder reached out and grabbed their throats. One golden tooth protruded as he smiled with delight at his ability to crash down doors of poor unsuspecting peasants. The gleam in his eye showed the enjoyment of his job all the more. "Papers, please, *prushalusta*!" he commanded in broken Russian. With no patience again he yelled "Papers!"

Bogdon scurried to the small metal table up against the kitchen wall. It had a drawer in it. He opened the drawer and pulled out his paperwork. It showed that he was a long-time resident in Kanev and his wife Svetlana of twenty-one years was also vindicated by these documents. Documents made out in the name of Mr. and Mrs. Bogdon Petroshenko. He pushed the other fake papers for the children to the back. He did not want to present them to the Germans because he did not want to take the chance that they might know that the papers were not authentic. Bogdon had them made up by his trusted friend Mr. Basansky who had an old printing press hidden in his cellar. Mr. Basansky also had other items that would be of interest to the resistance. Like all the extra food that he would share with others in the village that he trusted and for those who needed it most. Like the Petroshenko family.

The Officer glanced around the room as if sniffing something out. He looked at the small table and spoke ,"What else do you have in that drawer?"

"Nothing of interest, I am sure." Bogdon said with confidence, some anger almost showing through.

"If that is so, then you will not mind if I take a look?"

*As if I had a choice*, Bogdon almost thought aloud.

The dirty long fingernails of the German Officer accidentally pushed the papers back even further and a book presented itself and became his new point of interest.

"I see, hmm? What is this? It looks like a Bible to me." He yelled some obscenities in German and clicked his heels together.

His groveling assistant came running from behind the door and grabbed it from his commanding officer's hand. "You know what to do with this!"

"Yes sir! It will be a nice addition to our next book burning." Off the pawn ran into the darkness, grasping his new found treasure.

"You do know the penalty for having such a book in your home?" No answer, just stares came from the couple. "I could have you arrested this very night!" he bellowed out. "What do you think, this book of fairy tales is worth your life?" Still no answer and the couple just held each other and silently prayed.

Then a convenient disturbance came from the dark door. It was the pawn yelling, "We have found Jews down the street!" Just as quickly as the Nazis had come, they were suddenly gone.

A sigh of relief brought the couple's minds back to the four children, nestled snugly together in their night shirts, they continued to shiver in the cold blackness of the temporary pit. Bogdon removed the rug, lifted the trap door as Svetlana held the lantern for him.

"I do not think it will be safe for you to come out until morning. The Soldiers will be in town until late into the evening." Svetlana quickly tossed extra blankets down to the children. A tear streaked down her left cheek.

# Chapter 2

## The Box

The early morning light shone through the window pane and illuminated the area of the floor where the rug lay. Muddy boot prints littered the rustic wooden floor near the door and kitchen area as Larissa peered through the trapdoor from beneath. Slowly lifting it and steadying herself on the ladder, she felt that it was safe to come up. She looked over to the wooden rocking chair, near the fireplace. Svetlana had apparently dozed off. *She didn't even go to her own bed, she was so worried for our safety. How blessed we are to have her as a mother.*

The fifteen-year-old stumbled up the last step. A supple, smooth, and dark complexion gave a luster to her deep blue eyes. Flowing dishwater blonde hair, shiny and healthy. Unknowingly she was noticed by many of the young men in the village. One in particular had been smitten by Larissa since the day she came to live in the little town by the river.

"Come up Sasha." She kept her voice low. She did not want to wake her foster mother. Behind Larissa, Sasha pushed his dark locks aside and squinted as the light hit his wonderful round face. Sasha wore an off-white colored night shirt two sizes too big for a nine-year-old boy of his stature. Because he was a twin he always figured that his brother Alexi had at least half of his bodyweight. One thing Sasha was glad for was that Alexi was the smaller twin.

Trailing up behind the boys was perky little Anastasia with a button nose, bouncy light brownish hair and blue eyes that matched her older sister's. She was an exact replica of Larissa at that age. Anastasia yawned and gulped the early morning air of the small cabin and said, "I am hungry." It was loud enough to jar Svetlana from her peaceful position on the chair.

The sound of the creaking cabin door brought in Bogdon with more wood for the fire. "Ah, I see my family has survived another night in the pit." He said this half-jokingly with pain in his dark eyes. His face was worn yet not wrinkled. His eyes danced when he spoke to his newly-found children. He knew Svetlana always dreamed of a nice big family. With all the love in Bogdon's heart for his wife it became his dream too.

When they married so many years ago in days of lightness and peace, his heart skipped with joy every time he even glanced at his new bride. He loved her to the point of death and he knew nothing else mattered. He came from a loving family with strong values and traditions. His father gave him a Bible; inscribed inside their family tree. Not only did the Bible bring comfort and peace, but it held the family's roots. *It was a good thing that the book that was taken the other night was not a real Bible.* He thought to himself.

Bogdon remembered little Anastasia's wide-eyed curiosity about the "book" in the drawer when she first came to live with them. "What is that book called?"

"Actually, Dear One, it is not a book but rather a box that looks exactly like a Bible. See, when you open it, it stores valuable items like this." He held up a luscious red jewel.

"Wow, that is pretty. Where did you get it?"

"Yes, but not as pretty as you," he smiled. "Let me tell you a story."

*'There once was a Czar who was very kind and his wife, the Queen, who was even more kind. She invited all the peasants of this village to the palace for a dinner and gave each new bride a beautiful box that looked just like a Bible with a precious jewel in each. There were only five brides present there that night and your grandmother, Tamara, was one of them.'*

8

# CHAPTER 3

## BRINGING HOME JEWELS

Bogdon recalled the day he first met the four children. That day Bogdon was traipsing around in the forest for food. He came upon the children by the river, trying as they might, to catch a fish. He saw their gaunt, scrawny silhouettes up against the September setting sun. The clear sky indicated an extremely cold evening in store and he knew they would not make it through the night.

At the sight of Bogdon, Larissa had gathered the children under her wing like a mother hen gathers her chicks to protect them. The forest butted up to the river on one side, and the tall green lush grass flowed to the edge of the rushing waters on their side. As Bogdon stepped near, Larissa raised the homemade fishing pole with fear in her eyes. The pole was a stick with some string and a small hook at the end. She raised it up and determined to strike him if he came any closer.

"You need not be afraid." Bogdon said with a kind voice. "You will all come to my home and have dinner with me and my wife."

"I think you must know that we are Jewish, and you would be taking a big risk. How do I know you are not one of them?" She questioned him with apprehension.

"I am a Ukrainian villager." Bogdon said. "Most of our village is friendly to the Jews. Besides, I am a believer of the Word of God, Psalm 122:6 '…may they prosper who love* you…' Truly you do not need to fear." After much convincing and no fish on the hook, Larissa decided to take a chance. After all they had spent two nights in the forest hiding, starving and praying.

---

* (the Jewish people)

It was true that most of the villagers were friends to the Jews, but just to be on the safe side, they made up the story that the children were Bogdon's brother's from far-away Siberia. They had said that his brother lost his life in a railroad accident, and the mother was not able to care for them, so she put them on the train to Kanev. Along with the fake papers for the children, Mr. Basansky even fashioned a death certificate for Bogdon's poor bother: Peter Petroshenko.

After feeding the children, Svetlana doted on Larissa and knew exactly what a young girl might want after being on such a risky adventure. After all, she longed for the day when she could care for children. The claw-footed tub in a dark corner of the shed of their three-room home was a luxury indeed. Three wax candles dimly lit the room as Svetlana emptied the huge kettle of boiling water into the tub of cold well water to make it comfortable for her. Larissa's muscles went limp and she sighed heavily as she slipped into the warmth. She finally felt peace and safety. Each child took a bath after Larissa. Svetlana came up with mismatched pieces of clothing for the children to wear to bed that night. She would wash their clothes in the morning.

The extra room had a cot that served as Larissa's new bed. Blankets were piled on top of some straw in the corner for her little sister as well. The twin boys made do by the fireplace on the bare hardwood floor. To them it seemed comfortable and cozy with a down pillow they shared and a couple of old blankets Svetlana pulled from the attic. The tired boys dozed off quickly as Bogdon and Svetlana gazed on the sight of slumbering children in their home. With a gleam, their eyes met and it lit up the room with a warmth a fire could never bring. It felt so right to them. They went off to their own small bed and slept soundly.

Bogdon made sure that the boys had a room in the shed. He fashioned a wall of sorts with a large blanket that he had hung. He built a sturdy bed out of logs and twine and found a used mattress at a friend's house down the road. Another cot was purchased for Anastasia. All of the children felt at home with the sweet couple.

But, nevertheless, Anastasia questioned her sister. "When will we see our mama and papa again? Why do we have to stay here? When will we go home?"

"Sweetie," she said with the most tender voice possible, "we will not be returning to our home. Mama and Papa have gone to heaven; we now live with the Petroshenkos." The mention of her parents gave a lump to Larissa's throat, but she fought back the tears for Anastasia's sake. She needed to stay strong for the whole family.

# Chapter 4

## Brewing Romance

The day after the Nazis came and all the children were eating a bread-and-cheese breakfast, a tap came at the door. Everyone glanced at each other and then Larissa smiled, "It's for me." she said.

After last night's incident, Bogdon said protectively, "I'll get it." He opened the door. A rugged looking young man stood there holding some wild flowers he had picked along the side of the road. Bogdon smiled and said "Oh, for me? How nice of you to think of me."

Laughter from around the table came at the young man's expense. He bent down a bit to fit his tall, muscular body into the door. He smiled and looked toward Bogdon, "May I?"

"Oh, yes, please come in Maxime." Bogdon patted Maxime's huge frame and offered him breakfast.

Maxime approached Larissa. She batted her eyes in her shyness. She almost tipped the glass of milk setting before her. He awkwardly put the flowers in her face and said, "I-I plucked, I mean I picked these for you."

She blushed and held out her hands to grasp them and scooped them up. "Thank you, Max, how beautiful and thoughtful of you."

Maxime's face was glowing as his stomach did flips each time he looked in her eyes! To break the tension he spoke of the news he came to tell the family. "You know Mr. Basansky was taken into custody last night? It is very sad. He was caught with an extra chicken. They will take him to Kiev." Everyone knew the consequence for extra products. They had enjoyed many themselves from Mr. Basansky and so they sat in silence pondering their own fate. Although they were grateful they were spared yet another time, their hearts were heavy for their friend.

Maxime sat beside her on the long bench, but they did not say another word to each other throughout breakfast. All that he wanted to convey could not be said in front of this audience of teasers. He wanted to spill his heart to Larissa and tell her how much he wanted to be with her the rest of his life and to take care of her. But all this must wait until later when they might steal a moment away to talk.

# Chapter 5

## The Enemy's Nest

The brazen boots stomped once again in the nearby city of Kiev. Kiev, the capitol, was a large city and the same boots that had trailed through the small village last evening were now heading to an ancient building there. That building, draped in a large Swastika, headquartered the SS soldiers and Nazis that would give the weary marching men some relief. The building was one of many that the Nazis took the liberty of confiscating for their own use. The book burning was scheduled for that night in the town square nearby, and it seemed to spur on the behavior of the men.

Laughter echoed in the tall brick buildings lining the town square that housed the men of war as one soldier poured vodka. "Where is the tramp from the brothel?"

"Your turn is on the way. There are not enough to go around you know." His comrade slurred his speech as he swayed back and forth in a drunken stupor.

Buildings were not the only things that were confiscated for the personal use of this formidable enemy. While some women came willingly from the pubs and brothels, some of the women were brought against their will. They were young beautiful Ukrainian girls of age twelve and over. The fear in their eyes told a story in itself. Some were famished girls that were made a promise that they would be well fed and bathed so they went willingly. They did not know the evil they gave their souls over to. All for a hot meal and a bar of soap, but it was that or die starving.

# Chapter 6

## Ruby Found

Outside, a cattle car full of Jewish prisoners pulled up alongside the murky village square. Along with the marching men and the Commandant's vehicle, the procession made its way to the town square. Like a parade they marched up and stopped in front of a massive, mounting stack of banned literature, books, and papers of every kind.

"Achtung!" The Commandant bellowed. "I want to make it clear to all you Jews that this book burning should serve as a reminder to you of your own fate." His stern, harsh eyes were fierce with hatred as he spewed his words from hell. The interpreter followed suit and conveyed their coming demise. The crowd roared, clapped and cheered their approval. "Light the fire!" he roared as his eyes widened in a crazed trance. Again the wild crowd howled in delight.

An atmosphere of death hung over the cattle car, silence behind bars, masses of flesh pressed up against the windows of the vehicle. Packed so tightly, it was hard to imagine how one could even breathe in such a circumstance. The inhumane stench permeated the air. Yet blank stares from starving eyes continued to fixate on the town square from inside the truck. A smaller procession of a younger crowd, all with stars on their jacket sleeves, trailed behind the car. (A six-pointed star was place on the clothing of all who were Jewish so that they could be immediately recognized by the enemy.)

The little marchers looked to be between five and twelve. One little girl stood out in the large angry mob. She trudged by the fiery scene. Her feet were tired with blisters and the bitter cold nipped at her nose. She glanced up and saw towering flames with flickering embers reaching for the barren dark sky. She stared for some time as her mind filled with a wonderful thought. *Simmering hot borsht on mama's cook stove.* She stared until her sore neck jerked her back into reality.

Suddenly, she glanced across the fiery inferno and she caught sight of something a soldier had tossed. It cruised through the air, as if in slow motion, and tumbled down next to her right foot. She looked to the ground. She gazed in wonder at what appeared to be a book, meant for the fire, that had opened up directly underfoot. It wasn't a book though. It was a box. An opulent shiny red jewel tumbled out and landed at her feet. It's sparkle reflected the raging fire and caught her eye. She glanced around. No one seemed to be looking. Bending down, she scooped up the necklace and placed it in her warm wooly coat pocket. She smiled for the first time since she had been separated from her mother. A warmth came over her as the flames licked her face.

Her mother was bubbly and happy all the time. Little Tamara missed her so much even though she knew that mama was in the cattle car just ahead of her. They had been separated in the confusion. Tamara promised herself she would give the jewel to mother as soon as this scary walk in the dark was over. Her eyes grew heavy as the heat from the fire warmed her. Earlier they had been ordered to stop and she could not stand any longer. Her tiny legs gave way out from underneath her. Propping herself up against a post near a bush, she wandered off into a haze of sleepiness. Her last memory before falling asleep was the grip of her hand on the ruby jewel in her warm pocket.

# CHAPTER 7

## ESCAPE

She awoke to a cold shiver. Black soot covered her grey overcoat. Unaware that it also covered her face, she glanced about the area. No one was to be found anywhere. A clock tower rang five times echoing off the brick in the early morning darkness. The dank cold air enveloped her tiny being and her bottom lip began to quiver. A tear welled up in her eye as she realized that she was alone. She sat back in the safety of the bushes, held her dirty hands over her eyes and wept silently.

A single shadowy figure moved past the spot Tamara occupied. Involuntarily her whimpering increased, reaching the ears of the passerby. He knelt beside her and scooped the small child up almost as an instant reflex. The tiny body went limp from the devastation and crumpled into his arms.

He had to be careful because he had just escaped the clutches of the SS. *I must be insane*, he thought to himself as he ripped the star off of the child's overcoat. *If I get caught it will be the death of both of us, but if I stand by and do nothing death is certain.*

21

Mr. Basansky made his way toward the train station. He used the black of the night and the solitude of alleyways for cover. On and on he stepped, determined to get to safety, walking at a fast pace despite his labored breathing. "Okay little one, we're close now. We just need a miracle. We will just rest right here until the train comes"

He pressed his back on the three sided brick stoop that secretly housed them in perfect sight of the whistle stop. After what seemed like an eternity, the early morning train to Kanev chugged up to the train deck. "Whooo hooo." The whistle blew. Knowing that the train would leave immediately because there was only one lone silhouette that was waiting to board the train, Mr. Basansky scooped up the child once again and ran as fast as he could toward the tracks. In the shadows of nearby buildings, covertly he skipped the passenger part of the train and headed toward the caboose. Frantically he looked at each rail car to see if one had a door left open. Anxiety racked his entire aching body, but he could not find one single car door open. Suddenly, he stumbled and dropped the child. She let out what started to be expression of her pain, but he covered her mouth with his hand. "Shhhh, *prashulsta*, ssshh." She understood that she must be quiet.

"Whoo hoo!" The whistle blew, indicating the train's departure. The crescent moon came from behind the clouds for a moment. It was just long enough for him to see the only open door on the last car before the caboose. He fled toward it and hoisted the child up on the floor of the car. Just as the train began to pull away, he swiftly pulled himself up and lay on his back and let out a heavy sigh.

Mr. Basansky was a survivor and he was also now a savior to the small heap that lay curled up on the rough hewn wood floor of the train car. The train whistled out a tune and misty smoke puffed upward to rush by the open car door. The rustling wind blew through their hair. The morning sun peered over hillsides,

creating mist in the dawn. Sparse patches of wooded areas draped the landscape. The Ukraine became known long ago as the bread basket of the world. Its topsoil was forty feet deep. The panorama quickly passed them by as he resisted sleep. He must listen for the next whistle-stop and quickly get off the train.

He had no idea what he would do with the precious little life fate had put in his hands. They reached their destination without further incident. He simply waited for the stop and they jumped to safety. They hid behind the tree near the steppes until the one passenger had disappeared down the dirt road leading to the small town of Kanev. Mr. Basansky began to walk through the field opposite the train station, Tamara's legs having to work twice as hard to keep up. She did catch up and cusp her hand into his. His small one-room cabin came into view at daybreak. Home never looked so inviting. He tucked the weary child into his own bed and laid on the bearskin rug on his floor, near the fireplace.

# Chapter 8

## Tamara

At their home nearby, Bogdon was stretching himself after a short night's sleep. "Svetlana, I cannot sleep, I keep thinking I must check on Mr. Basansky's animals and belongings."

"I am in agreement. If it was not for him we would not have survived last winter. Go and be safe," she said as she rolled back over to snooze a bit more.

Bogdon's knuckles wrapped at Mr. Basansky's door in the early morning light brightening the skyline. Crisp fresh air filled Bogdon's lungs as he exhaled a heavy sigh. Again he tapped out a quick token knock. He expected no answer. He peered cautiously through the partially curtained window. He pushed open the door slowly, revealing a fear-filled face. Then he sighed with relief at the sight of a friend.

"What are you doing here? How did you get here? No matter, you need to leave quickly. They will return for you and this is the first place they will look." Bogdon belted out the myriad of exasperating questions and statements.

"Who is that?" The small voice squealed from behind the door before Mr. Basansky could get his bearings.

With a puzzled look on his face, Bogdon pushed open the door further to reveal the beautiful gem of a child standing there, filthy, worn and tired.

"What do we have here?" He said with a loving smile.

"It is a sign of my true insanity," said Mr. Basansky sheepishly.

"Well, now for sure you both will come to my home and we will make do until we find a better place for both of you."

"Thank you but *nyet*," said the grateful man. "I could never do that to you and your wife. You have enough apples in your basket."

"Well, for sure if you stay here you will not only put yourself in danger but this child as well." Bogdon looked into the little one's eyes. "What is your name, sweetie?"

The little one flushed with embarrassment and spoke in the smallest of voices, "Tamara."

"What a beautiful name. That was my mother's name you know." Tamara smiled bigger. There was something about this child that he could not quite put his finger on but he must make sure of her safety.

Bogdon insisted Mr. Basansky come with him, but he refused. "If I cannot live without fear, then should I live at all? I will stay."

Suddenly realizing Mr. Basansky's nocturnal heroics, he inquired, "But how on earth did you get away?"

"I was set free miraculously last night. There was a book burning and the soldiers were all overworked and had a few too many rounds of vodka. Especially the one that happened to be guarding our cell. He fell asleep, and since he was right outside my cell, I waited until everyone was deep asleep. I took the key and fled, then I stumbled across the little one."

"Please, *prashulsta*, I beg of you to come." Yet he could see there was no convincing him. "At least let me take the child, I know we do not have the room but we have the food and the love."

"*Da, da*, of course you must take the child."

Bogdon gave his friend a worried but grateful look and off they went, the little one under his arm, once again bringing home a child for his family to love.

# CHAPTER 9

## ANOTHER JEWEL

Anastasia's nose was pressed against the window, waiting for her papa to return. Then in the distance, just beyond the large oak that shaded the lane leading to their yard, he came. *But what was this?*

Anastasia's forehead wrinkled in thought. "Mama, Mama!" yelled the little one with delight. "Papa has someone with him." Then all the little faces peered through the misty window pane with a bewildered look.

"*Da*! Mama look!" said Sasha with a smile on his face.

As Bogdon and Tamara approached, Svetlana told the children, "Be kind to this new child. We do not know what she has been through." Each child there just seemed to know how to welcome Tamara with open arms. They had learned well from the Petroshenkos. Anastasia ran out to pick some of the earliest blooming flowers near the oak tree then continued to run up to Tamara and said, "This is for you!" with a welcoming smile.

"*Spasiba!*" a wide-eyed Tamara whispered. Anastasia took her by the hand and walked her home.

Tamara felt loved and wanted in her new home and even though she longed for her mother, she would do her best to fit in here.

The same afternoon that she came to live with the beautiful mismatched family and found two new sisters and two new brothers, Tamara understood that she would never see her own mother again. She knew this from all the conversations she had overheard, and all the talk her own mother had tried to protect her from. Nonetheless she heard it. She knew of the permanent separations and even of the deaths. She would only allow herself to think of her mother in a positive light, like the bubbly person she was. She also overheard Larissa repeat the account of Mr. Basansky to Svetlana. He was not as fortunate as little Tamara, he was returned to custody that very night and not heard from again.

# CHAPTER 10

## DEATH AND NEW LIFE

A few trusted townspeople gathered at their home. Bogdon spoke some solemn words as they bowed their heads and brushed tears of sorrow from their eyes. "Mr. Basansky had a heart for the people, God rest his soul. He will be greatly missed." Bogdon cleared his throat. He glanced up at the small gathering and looked towards the door. They knew without speaking that they must leave. Any more of an assembly and they would have called attention to themselves. One by one each mourner silently left.

A happier gathering would ensue in just a few short months. Maxime had finally conjured up the courage to let Larissa know how he felt. She had so much fear in her the day he asked her to marry him. She spent a restless night tossing and turning for she had confessed her love back to him as well and accepted his invitation. They were now engaged. But the love confession was not the problem. The problem was that she had not yet told him that she was Jewish. *How would Maxime feel about her once he knew? Would he take back his vows? Could she live with herself if she just didn't tell him at all? What if he found out after they were married or worse yet after they had children?* She could wait no longer. Even though it was before sunrise, the next morning she ran all the way to his cottage at the end of the lane near the river bank. She rapped on the door. "Max," her voice wavered.

"What is it Larissa, what's wrong, you look terrified."

"I have a confession to make." Her eyes looked at the ground. "I am..." she hesitated, "Jewish."

A huge smile came across Maxime's face. "Oh, is that all? Don't you think I knew that? Come here." He held out his large arms and pulled her in and cradled her.

# CHAPTER 11

## THE WEDDING

It was in the end of June when Larissa and Maxime were wed. The whole town attended the joyous occasion. There was never much reason to celebrate during those trying times, but when there was a good reason, they celebrated wholeheartedly. Anastasia and Tamara were dressed in their prettiest dresses made with calico and lace. Bogdon and the twins looked handsome in their vested woolen suits with bow ties. Svetlana wore a white smock over an older, but nice dress she kept in her closet for just such an occasion. The gown that she had worn for her own wedding was tailored to fit Larissa. Off white in color, it had long sleeves and a high neck with lace and bead work all around the bodice. The groom stood at the altar wearing a borrowed black suit that seemed just a bit too big on him. When he caught a glimpse of his bride coming down the aisle his eyes opened wide. He beamed with pride.

Anastasia and Tamara wiggled and even giggled a bit through the ceremony. Tamara, only one year older than Anastasia, halted it before it got out of hand. Tamara wanted to show her appreciation for being so welcomed into this family. It was so nice of Larissa to let her be a flower girl along with Anastasia.

The atmosphere was filled with the love of family and friends as they made their vows one to another before God and man. Beaming with joy, Larissa kissed her groom as the marriage was solidified. Smiles rose inside the hearts of the small crowd gathered there that day, celebrating a rare joyous event in such trying times at the beginning of WWII in a stoic Eastern Block nation.

# CHAPTER 12

## A CHRISTMAS GIFT

It had been eight months since Tamara had come to stay with the Petroshenko household. She was growing and flourishing in health as well as spirit. The family had gathered in the tiny front room where Bogdon had brought in a small Christmas tree from the forest. He took out his Bible and read the account in the book of Saint Luke about the birth of Jesus. A warm unified feeling came over the entire family as embers flickered in the stone fireplace as Bogdon read:

*Luke 2:4-7 KJV*

*4 And Joseph also went up from Galilee, out of the city of Nazareth, into Judaea, unto the city of David, which is called Bethlehem; (because he was of the house and lineage of David:)*

*5 To be taxed with Mary his espoused wife, being great with child.*

*6 And so it was, that, while they were there, the days were accomplished that she should be delivered.*

*7 And she brought forth her firstborn son, and wrapped him in swaddling clothes, and laid him in a manger; because there was no room for them in the inn.*

After Bogdon finished the family settled in together comfortably in the cozy cabin. Larissa snuggled ever closer to her new husband Maxime. They could not take their adoring eyes off of each other. The twins fidgeted with the small wooden soldiers Bogdon had fashioned out of a branch for them. They had never once received a gift in their lives and now this was too much for them to bear. Anastasia danced about the room, dress swirling up then down, hair flying and face beaming with joy. She clutched the homemade rag doll Svetlana had put together the night before. The other doll for Tamara was still in its box under the tree.

Tamara stood staring at the tree. She had not seen such a sight ever. It was simply decorated with candles and with white strips of cloth that were tied into bows. Her eyes twinkled in thought. Suddenly, she darted off to her room. The room had been furnished with a trundle bed. With Larissa betrothed and no longer there, there was room for both girls. She lifted the loose floor board in the corner of the room and pulled out a small black bag drawn shut with string. She held it close and ran out to her new parents and stretched forth the bag. Eyes dancing with excitement she blurted out, "Happy Christmas to you both. I love you."

They did not expect this at all. A tear came to Svetlana's eye and a lump to the throat of Bogdon. They smiled and Svetlana held the weighted bag in her rough left hand, moving it up and down with a questioning look on her face.

"Please, *prushalsta* open it Mama!"

With every eye in the room on Svetlana she pulled the strings, parted the material, wider and wider the mouth of the bag was opened. Tipping the little sack upside down, out slid the long lost Ruby red jewel! Bogdon's awe filled eyes met Svetlana's. "This cannot be so! Is this Mama's Royal Red Ruby?"

They knew they had done the right thing by keeping "just one more child" in their small cramped home. One more "Gem" to love and raise. They picked up the small child and smothered her in hugs and kisses. They had their Jewel, they had their Bible and they had each other. All was well.

Bogdon picked up the Bible and the black pen next to it. He began to inscribe the names of each child onto the family tree inside the front page of the Bible.

**Ukraine**

# About the Author

Little Fawn Whitecedar is a Native American author and resident of Northern Michigan's lower peninsula. She is a Christian first and foremost and is married to Gary, and both are very involved in their local church. She has three adult children Ann, Joshua and Amy and a dog named Rufus .

Having traveled to the country of the Ukraine on three different occasions, Whitecedar felt this story just fall, as a download from heaven, unto the page as she wrote it . Also having researched extensively the area, and calling on Ukrainian friends that are interpreters, has helped make this work of Historical Fiction come to life. She long felt it needed to be read by more than just a few people and is very pleased that it is finally being published!

As a former news writer for a local newspaper and the Army National Guard. Whitecedar has had many experiences and stories she would love to share.

# Intentions

The intent of this first published book is to take half of any proceeds made by the author and give them to a non-profit organization that the author is very passionate about: That is to help end a world epidemic problem of the sex trafficking of little children and women around the world.

If you liked this book and would like to buy copies for your friends and simultaneously help with a worthy cause please go to either Westbow Printing Press, Amazon.com, or Barns and Noble for further information on ordering for your e-reader. You just may save or change someone's life while doing so. Thank you.

The following is a sample of Little Fawn's next book: Chapter 1-

# White Cedar
By Little Fawn Whitecedar
Based on a true story.


# THE BIRTHING

September 1, 1930. Writhing pain wracked her whole body, streams of sweat began to slide down her entire being as she held in, with all her might, the inevitable shriek that must come. Her chest pulsating up and down, up and down, like air being forced out and drawn back in from a fire stoker. The beads of water that trickled down her back caused a suction to the steely cold metal table each time she sat up and heard the unfamiliar voice yell "Push!"

Flashes of serious faces, bright lights, combined with the sounds of sanitized metal clinking together caused a dizzying effect. She glanced down to her huge stomach. She heard the command again, "Push!"

Chilled hands grasping her knees and spreading them apart again, echoing the same sentiment over and over, "Push, push, pusssssssssssh!"

"Aaaaaaaaaghhhhh!" came a gruntal utterance from her petite mouth. Dark eyes tightly shut crinkling an otherwise stoic bronze face. Long black hair wrapped about her neck as warm hands from behind pull it back to help bring relief in her most distressful moment.

"It's okay, Katherine, breathe, breathe, lie back now." whispered the only voice of comfort heard thus far.

Lying back, stuck against the metal table, saturated in sweat, anointed with heat and wracked with pain, she sighed. Taking in a deep breath and turning her head and rolling her eyes upward they met with that of the one who had been consoling her. The Nurse's deep blue eyes smiled and for a brief moment of forgotten pain, eyes slowly closing, Katherine felt a peace, as these eyes took her back home so far away on the Reserve.

*Nostrils filled with the sweet aroma of spring flowers as the long blades of grass tickled her knees, she giggled to herself. Strolling along the bank of the rock laden creek a fluttering blue bird comes into view as it floats by and blocks, for only a moment, the beautiful rays of sunshine reflecting the creek bed, warmed her bronze face.* Darkness.

Suddenly as if being ripped from a pleasant dream, Katherine is jerked back into reality. Sitting bolt up right, drenched with droplets of labor, a sweat puddle had formed on the table at her lower back. She gave an ancient resounding tribal shriek that echoed off the harsh brick walls.

Emerging eruption at last came, relieving the suffering of her entire body. Heart pounding with so much expectation, still the heavy breathing continues but with less labor. Sweet wailing sounds coo from the arms of the consoling nurse, smiles on each attendants face give assurance that all is well.

Outstretched arms, flail forth to embrace the tiny wonder as a single tear slowly trickles from Katherine's eye, "It's a boy." she uttered in a hushed tone to herself.